THE THINGS FATHER DID NOT TEACH US

ABIMBOLA O. ALAKA

First published in Great Britain as a
softback original in 2021

Copyright © Abimbola O. Alaka
The moral right of the author has been asserted.
All rights reserved.

No part of this publication may be reproduced, stored in a retrieval system, or transmitted, in any form or by any means, without the prior permission in writing of the author, nor be otherwise circulated in any form of binding or cover other than that in which it is published and without a similar condition including this condition being imposed on the subsequent purchaser.

Cover Design: Buzzdesignz

Published by 'The Roaring Lion Newcastle'
ISBN: 978-1-913636-88-3

Email:
books@theroaringlionnewcastle.com

Website:
www.theroaringlionnewcastle.com

Dedication

Dear Dad,

This book is dedicated to you. Thank you for being my hero, thank you for being selfless, caring, and loving 'till death.
I have written this book to encourage younger people out there so that they don't have to succumb to the pressures of the outside world.
You have always told me to be true to myself.
It hurts that you're not here to pat me on the back.
I am sure you're proud of me and are ready to tell everyone who cares to hear that your baby has a book.

Rest well, Papa!

Table of Contents

Acknowledgements

Delving into book writing is harder than I thought, but fulfilling. This makes it all worth the effort, time, money, and sacrifices that have gone into it.

A special thank you to my husband. Thank you for being supportive, encouraging me and holding my hands. You're the best, my love. To my kids, thank you for going to bed earlier than usual so I could concentrate. I love you so, so much.
To my family: thank you for the support.

I want to acknowledge the reader, too. Thank you for believing in and supporting me by reading my book.

Sincere thanks to Tolu' A. Akinyemi ("Lion of Newcastle") and everyone on my publishing team. I would also like to say a big thank you to the editor, Diane Donovan, for an exceptional job.

To all the teenagers dealing with one or more societal pressures, take a deep breath and know that you're not alone. Keep striving hard, and become the best version of yourself. When life puts you in tough situations, don't say **"why me?"** Just say, **"try me."**

POEMS

The Socratic Way to Die

Here,
You are a rebel.
Your rebellion? Too many questions.
You are pushed away, exiled
When you see a mystery.
You can't see a word.
Here, a question is a crime.
If you cannot run, shy away.
Talk to the wind.
Keep the doors of your lips shut.
Curiosity killed the cat;
It killed Socrates, too.
It killed creativity in our classroom;
It led free men to their doom.
I asked,
Are all gay men evil?
The congregation nailed me to the cross,
Bi-Jesus;
Crucified my mind.

The Things Father Did Not Teach Us

We sat in twos, threes, and fours
under the tree of life, for the things
our father taught us:
empathy, bravery, love, and thoughtfulness.

In life,
to be brave,
you carry your shoulders high,
lift your chin, empty the river in your eyes, and,
like troubled dust, you rise.
To be brave, you fold your fears into the
Titanic and watch it drown in your tears.

In life, to love,
you forget yourself,
selfishness, and everything that makes another feel
less.

In life,
to be thoughtful,
you become a library.
You are patient.
If you embrace solitude
and watch your thoughts become pictures,
wisdom will ooze out of your words.

Self-Declaration (For The Girl Child)

(say after the poet:)

I am beautiful.

I am smart.

I am strong.

I am a woman.

I am a Queen.

My heart is a gold mine,

Home of good things,

And my smile comes naturally

Like the omen of goodwill.

I am fierce.

I am lioness.

I am full of strength.

I am worthy.

I am significant.

I am at peace with myself.

I am amazing.

You Versus the World

Like death, mistakes are inevitable
And when you fall,
you don't build a tent in the mud.
You stand.
You walk.
You run.

You're gold—
Carry yourself like royalty,
Value yourself than anyone else,
Process your fears; have self-belief

Instead of a trembling heart.
Fight your fears face to face,
'Cause everything good is
on the other side, and it takes courage to get there.

Brace up!
You're the walls of your heart.
You are your truth,
And the rest of the world is a lie.

When the Rest of the World is Against You

Squinting in the mist,
Piercing through the fog,
You're betwixt two,
Yourself and the rest of the world.
You're young and agile,
And when they push you,
Remember: you carry strength within you.

You're special,
And the rest of the world is only blind to not see it.
You're a wonder;
You don't need to prove it.
When the world is against you,
Don't bend.
Chin up.
Stand tall.
You're not lonely if you stay alone;
You stand out.
And they can't wrap their mind around that.

A Poem In Which My Silence Is Seen As Everything Stupid

Because my tongue doesn't taste the rhythm
of the air, nor does my mouth march the lies from
your lips;
Because I do not do drugs or caress alcohol
like you do;
Because I embrace myself and chill with the angels
in my head;
Because I built a barricade between us, doesn't
make me a fool. It doesn't mean your blows should
sleep in my skin. It doesn't mean your insults should
wrap my *awakening*.

Struggle for Self-Portrait

"To be yourself in a world that is constantly trying to
make you someone else is the greatest achievement."
~Ralph Waldo Emerson

my ears have become

a field of insults that feast like

fireflies; a carpet where consonants

cluster. They say virginity is

immaturity; they say unfolding

my faith is the path to peace, until

I wrestled and wrestled with thoughts

and finally followed them. My ardent

desire was to be a friend; to be played with.

My ardent desire was to feel loved...until

the truth heaved my shoulders into embracing

myself and feeling happy even when sadness

lurked at the corner.

How Easy

it is for criticisms to ravage one
'till he gleams black. How easy it is for
insults to build best in one's head 'till
he becomes unsettled like ripples; like reoccurring
waves; like Nigerian news; like...
How easy it is for a flavoured heart to
metamorphose into a mural of aches
if one isn't blocked from the criticisms;
if one doesn't fix his eyes on the future.

A Poem: I Hate The Shelter of Society

tears are shedding their crispy skin down the drift of
my face in this

darklit room, and i snap them off— i do not want to
taste the shadow of

sadness; nor do i want grief's cold embrace.

i hate it. i hate them!

my mouth is metamorphosing into a horse of insults.
my heart is shooting

anger. it's shooting grief and failure, grief and failure,
all over; but

i try to let hope sail me away. i do not want to cradle
the mischief crawling into

my loins. i try to let hope sail me away. i do not want
to taste the shadow

of sadness! i do not! i hate it. i hate them!

i try to pull out the pains triggered into my sinews
and unbutton anxiety, but they grow wings like a
falcon. I was passing by when some guys molested

me. Indignation/disappointment/resentment wove
my heart into a tower of dust. why have

molestations/rapes/sexual assaults sheltered
society? why has she become an autocrat?

the fan above is still muttering. i do not want to feel
grief's cold embrace, so i try to let hope sail me away.

one day, she'll lose her crown to the wind.

Do Not Pretend

Do not pretend you know the grief in this skin;

the pain in my veins. Do not pretend you didn't throw

insults at my face, made you rage, interrupted my pace.

Do not pretend to throw peace-deprivation or self-depreciation.

You said virginity is stupidity—said that calmness is weakness

'till I walked in a worldliness that later led to worthlessness.

You saw the Earth as a catalogue of choice, made a wrong

choice, and forced me to do the same. I blame myself. I blame

myself for chewing your lies; for chewing the life you chose.

You saw guys as flirt-flies, perched on many of them, and forced

me to do the same. Now that pregnancy is breaking me bit by bit.

Do not pretend you know the regret I live in; the pain in my veins.

In The Blue-Blanketed Morning

my memory unrolls the number of dating proposals

from those that claimed to love me, and fear rattles

my intestines again. Pressure barrels from my pores

again. I've run from them; hid from them; tried building

a barricade; but they still keep chasing me, like cheetahs.

Fear rattles my insides again. Pressure barrels from my pores

again, and fatigue finds an escape route from my head. I've run and run,

hid and hid, but they keep chasing me like cheetahs. They say I'm the sun

that spreads smile on their faces. They say my beauty can burn a whole house.

Instead of believing their lies or ruminating their praises, I'll emphasize my "no"

and keep up with my goals.

Where The Wheel Reaches

the wheel reaches where three statues are
whispering

to the wind in Lagos state, and a sigh sifts

my shoulder into sadness. say, a girl breaks like a
discouraged cloud when the wheel reaches where
three statues are whispering

to the wind in Lagos state. the wind replays the
scenarios in my parents' house and i try to unbuckle
the hurts housing my throat, but they cleave

like a nail in wood. i'll soon be in a house where
insults and fists are the synonyms

for greetings. Father would mould Mother into a
chimney

of tears and Mother would throw curses at him.
Father's fists would go hungry

and feast on Mother's skin 'till the remains of her
insults hid in her lips.

It has made me hide in the dark and love depression.
It has made me sink in inferiority,

nurse stillness, and has made self-hatred my best
friend. It has made me

unfurl my faith in God, and hate my parents. But I'll carry my cross and cry for self-love,

self-esteem, and everything that breathes joy.

Choosing Love Over All Odds

Each day, the monster of pains boiling with
rage and hate gazes at my face, trying to flip
a feather of tears into my pupils.

Each day, depression tries to sink
my shoulder into debris; each day it
tries to wallow me in the river of shame.

I wriggle myself to joy; allow nightingales
to flutter in my mouth. I empty my pot of pain
and fight my fears as a warrior of Troy. I

allow my sincerest laughter to flow like
a crystal stream and echo like the chirp of a skylark.
I allow self-acceptance and love to elevate me, and I
flip and flap into success.

There's Nothing

"You're the worst child I've ever had!"
still grows wings in my head. The draining
it reads; the emptiness...the worthlessness, the...
There's nothing as gnawing a chimney of rejection
from Mother's mouth. There's nothing!
There's nothing that fades with depression; with
dislikes.
There's really nothing as hard as bearing glowing
grief beneath the skin. Mother said I'm the worst
child, and I find myself picking dead leaves; hiring in
shells. I pray and still pray that God sends the wind
to sweep this hurt from my heart.

Salvation

The day the night held the sun by her neck
And threatened to slaughter her like Fulani
herdsmen;
The day the night paraded the Earth as a model
And scared the trees, the wind, the birds, and the
animals
To their shells;
When I was tasting the rhythm of my heartbeat,
Love revealed Himself; crept from my fingers
Through my pores/moisture/sinews/cells
To my heart
As my sins broke and caught me in redemption's
feet.

The Engineer of Success

Life became a mural of gloom
and grief when death wove Mother and Father
into towers of dust and
threw them into the sea. His labyrinth still teethes
so hard on my skin that it breaks like the beak of a
red-feathered hen.
What is loss, if not the unfolding of grief and hunger?
The wandering wind wove Mother into an
exhausted moth and threw her into the waves, and
I couldn't but give my knees to the road for
redemption; but
neglect and jest drill into my heart so deeply that the
crumbs of their insults
still fall from my pores.
Instead of wallowing in
their rejections or drowning in poverty,
I roll away the laziness thumping in me and climb to
work.
For work is the engineer of greatness.

Had It Been

Had it been that love was the language we spoke,
the air we breathed, the refuge we sought—
Had it been that love was the aura we longed for;
hatred wouldn't have been the norm and peace
wouldn't have been in pieces.

A Haiku

room gleams in colours
others stand at attention —
Africa's beauty!

Words From Your Mother

Child,
if the whirling wind roars and you shiver and
fall like a bird soaked in blood;
if she blows ashes to your soul so that only odes
fall from your lips;
if she lunges and your fears and tears flow like
the Atlantic Ocean,
please, don't let regrets be the
anaesthesia for your skin.
Don't crash hope into the concrete,
for you have the might to rise again.

Yearning

My mind still frolics and lingers

at your personality and image—

beauty for beauty and roses for roses.

It births longing—births craving to have you in

my arms; births desire; births everything that calls
you.

It yearns for a garden where other voices

are beneath. Yearns for a place, sprinkling gardenia
and fragrance. It yearns. It craves. It cries, "come,
come" like a routined crow.

Won't you quench this thirst with your embrace?

When You Like a Girl

Every girl is a garden
full of color and beauty.
Tread carefully,
for angels watch over them.
When you like a girl,
don't flirt with her.
Dress well.
Wear your brightest smile.
Could you walk up to her?
Say that you want to be her friend,
a listening ear, and dearest dear.
Say that you'll be there to gear her up
on days when life kicks her down.
Say that you'll be peace-
gentle, kind, and sweet.
"Think about it."
Then walk away in style.

SHINE

Admit it!
You have a sweet soul.
Your heart is comely, soft, and peaceful; you are
magical.
Don't let the hurts get to you—
You're caring, and that's a rare gift.
Shine your light.
Don't stink!
The fragrance that erupts from your insides
Is the scent of kindness and compassion.
With you, Love is a verb.
Don't stop the flow.
Shine your light.
Never regret it!
When your good deeds sting you,
Don't let the pain push you away.
You're a rare breed.
Shine your light.

PRAYERS

Darling,
I pray you find happiness;
the kind that erases the memories of sadness;
that makes your face brim with smiles;
that makes you a firefly
and, like the sun, fills you with perfect light.
I pray that you find so much happiness—
more than enough to share.
Darling,
I beg that your smiles never shrink;
that you have enough bones to never to give up;
that the odds always be in your favour;
and that you live a life full of love.

THE NEXT TIME YOU GET LOST, FIND YOURSELF.

(This is not a poem)

At 16, six boys taught her how to use drugs. Her parents were there the whole time, but their hearts were a million miles away. They couldn't see, and she didn't reach out. At 16, she allowed lying lips to push her into a room full of smoke and needles, teaching her to love pain;

to get high on stuff that tastes like bile. Her life was lonely, like dark clouds hovering over a street that has no lamps. She blamed everyone else but herself and her friends, and the first time she felt high, it was like all the gods, the heavens, and hell were within her.

The thing is, life's not going to be perfect. It's a crazy curve. And the wall between you and your happiness are your demons. The next time you get lost, take a new turn, one step in the right direction. Find yourself.

SERENITY

What if
You shut out the noise
And focus on your insides,
Your thoughts, and everything that lies within?
What if
You let go of what no longer serves you,
Relationships that are toxic to you,
And leave it all
For your peace?
Please,
Embrace serenity.
Think your thoughts.
Enjoy your space.
Shut out the noise,
And focus on your insides.
You'll win.

THE TRUTH IN SEVEN LINES

You are special.

You are enough.

You don't need to fit in.

You are a perfect fit.

You are amazing.

You are beautiful.

Darling, you're perfect.

PUZZLE

why do you run
in circles, cycling
on whirling roads
littered with broken bottles?
why do you
call yourself names
that sound like an exclamation
and become fire when
someone says you're living a lie?
why do you
lead yourself to dark rooms
without windows and choke yourself?
why do you pretend
that you're happy
when you sleep every night with a heavy heart?
Catch yourself; you're drifting away.
Wake up and solve this puzzle.

Letter to My 16-Year-Old Self

Dear Self:
You're probably wondering
about who you are
and what you want to do with your life,
wandering in uncertainties.
You don't know what you want.
Excusing yourself from reality,
you are tossed around by peers.
Here and there, you flow like the beads on a dancer's
hips.
I know how it feels.
I've been to you.

Now,
I wish I read more books
then I played games;
played with myself more
then I played with friends.
I wish I'd followed my heart
and not what people said.
I wish I was quiet, reserved,
and paid attention to my thoughts.

Dear Self:

you're special.
discover your
uniqueness early;
do not flip around
like the pages of a boring book.
Find yourself,
and when you do,
love yourself.

Yours Faithfully,
Yourself.

THE NEXT TIME YOU FEEL LIKE GIVING UP

life is a mountain
most give up climbing.
not you. not you.
the next time you feel like
giving up,
squeeze your fist tightly,
close your eyes,
and say:
Not today. Not tomorrow. Not ever.

SELF-DECLARATION (2)

(with your right palm on your chest, read this aloud, slowly...)

Soft, full of light,

I am loving.
Taking no offense, I'm forgiving.

The world is lucky to have me.

I am bold.

I am confident.

I am destined to achieve great things.

Bio

Abimbola Ojurongbe-Alaka

is a creative writer and an HR consultant; a graduate of English studies from Babcock University, Ilishan Remo, Ogun State, and the University of Sheffield, UK.

She is a focused HR professional with a successful track record in recruitment, change management and the transformation of HR departments and organisations.

She was a National Winner of the Nigerian Stock Exchange essay competition in 2005.

When not writing, Abimbola spends her time baking pastries, sweets, and cakes.

Author's Note

Thank you for the time you have taken to read this book. I hope you enjoyed the poems in it.

If you loved the book and have a minute to spare, I would appreciate a short review on the page or site where you bought it. I greatly appreciate your help in promoting my work. Reviews from readers like you make a huge difference in helping new readers choose a book.

Thank you!
Abimbola O. Alaka